The FIDORI TRILOGY

BOOK 3:
THE JOURNEY TO THE TOP OF THE TREES

BY JASMINE FOGWELL

The Journey to the Top of the Trees
Book 3 of The Fidori Trilogy
Jasmine Fogwell
© Copyright 2016 By Jasmine Fogwell

Published by Destinée Media: www.destineemedia.com
Written by Jasmine Fogwell: www.jasminefogwell.com
Illustrations and cover illustration by Amanda Kramer Kaczynski
Interior design by Julie Lundy: www.juliekaren.com
Cover design by Devon Brown: www.oxburger.wix.com/oxburger

ISBN: 978-1-938367-27-4

Dedication

This book is dedicated to Blake Allen. Together, we created the creatures called Fidoris and I could not have written this book without him.

~

Pronunciation Key

Some of the names in this book have been inspired by my time in a small village in the Swiss Alps. Pronounce them as you wish, but this is how they sound when I tell the story!

Rionzi: RYE-on-zee

DuCret: DEW-cray

Nemesté: NEM-es-tay

Fidoris: fi-door-ees

BE SURE TO READ ALL OF

The FIDORI TRILOGY

BOOK 1:
AN UNLIKELY FRIENDSHIP

BOOK 2:
THE PURPLE FLOWER

BOOK 3:
THE JOURNEY TO THE
TOP OF THE TREES

BOOK 3:
THE JOURNEY
TO THE TOP
OF THE TREES

~

THE FIDORI TRILOGY · 2

A Fidori in Nemesté

imputus was not far behind the four companions as they crept back into Nemesté. When she returned to the cave and discovered Zintar gone, she had made her way to an opening in the trees that overlooked the village. She had spent many days and nights in this very spot, hating the villagers. They had taken everything that was important to her, and she vowed to haunt them as long as she lived. Now they had done it again by stealing her Fidori. She stroked a purple flower that sprouted up beside her, putting all the poison she could in it as she watched the village sleep peacefully.

Meanwhile, down in Nemesté, Rionzi, James, and Saleem snuck the strange Fidori into the apartment on the third floor of the old inn.

"James, you must go home," Mrs. DuCrét said. "Your parents will be worried sick."

He had skipped school all day, and it was now late in the evening. His parents were probably worrying and might have been searching for hours. He nodded and took off, and as he wandered across the village, lit only by the glow of the streetlights, he was afraid to even imagine what kind of trouble he might be in.

"James!" The familiar voice of his mother rang through the crisp air.

James turned around quickly and waved. He really didn't know what to do, so he smiled and said, "Hi."

She gave him a big hug, and he could tell by her swollen eyes that she had been crying for a long time. "Where have you been?" Her voice was mixed with anger and relief. "When you didn't come home from school, we started to worry. We called the school, and they said you weren't there all day, but I put you on the bus in the morning. Where have you been?" she said again, this time with a bit more anger than concern in her voice.

The longwinded explanation of his mother's worries had given him time to think through his response. He decided he didn't want to lie, but he wasn't going to tell the whole truth, either. He would deal with the punishment he was likely to receive. "Mom, I went to the forest all day," he said. "I'm sorry. I know I shouldn't have, and I should have told you where I was going."

Bella was taken aback a little by his answer. She hadn't been expecting such an honest and apologetic response. She began to weep again. "Oh, James, you shouldn't have gone. We've been worried sick. Why would you do that?"

"I don't know." That part was a lie. "I just did."

His mother had to laugh a little at his stern response. "James, I'm just so relieved you're safe. You'll be punished—you can't run off like that—but I'm so happy you're here." She reached for him and gave him another suffocating hug. His mother's arms wrapped around him were comforting, taking away some of his anxiety about the consequences of his actions.

His father wasn't so warm. "Son," he said sternly when they walked in the door. "Go to your room."

Bella reluctantly let go of James, who silently did as his father had asked. As he wandered up the stairs, he heard the beginnings of an argument between his parents.

"David, really, you could have acted a bit more relieved to see him," Bella argued.

"Bella, I am relieved, but he needs to understand the severity of pulling a stunt like that. He can't just wander off into the forest to play with imaginary friends while we have half the village worrying about him."

Their conversation went on for over an hour. James quietly shut his door so he didn't have to listen to it. He knew what he had done seemed wrong to them, and they had every right to be angry, but they didn't understand. It was confusing for him because he didn't know how to make them understand without telling them about Zintar, and he couldn't bring himself to do that. He didn't trust them enough. They probably wouldn't believe him, anyway, just as they hadn't before. There was too much at risk now if he said anything.

A light tap on his bedroom door startled him out of his thinking.

"James." His father's stern voice came through the door, though it had softened a bit since he had first come home. "Would you come downstairs, please? Your mother and I would like to speak with you."

"Yes, Father, I'll be right down." James waited till he heard his father reach the last step. Then he made his way down to the living room to accept his punishment.

Two lamps lit the room with a pleasant glow. David sat in one chair, and Bella sat on the long couch. He could feel their eyes glaring at him before he looked up. When he finally caught a glimpse of both their faces, he realized they had both been crying. He was a little surprised, because his dad had been so angry, but when he looked again to see, he was pretty certain his eyes were red and swollen. There was also a pile of tissues overfilling the waste basket. James wanted to cry, too, knowing he had caused his parents so much grief, but he held back because he knew he had to be brave in facing his punishment.

"James, I'm not sure where to start." David broke the awkward silence. "Your mother and I are very shaken up over what happened today. Do you have anything you'd like to say?"

"I shouldn't have done it," James muttered meekly.

"Then why did you?" David asked.

"I don't know," James lied.

"James, you understand you can't disappear like that without some consequences?" His father seemed to be asking for some sort of explanation.

"Yes, sir" was all James said.

"If you don't have anything else to say, your mother and I have decided to ground you from the forest for a month."

James couldn't hold his tears back any longer. "Yes, sir," he said with a sniffle.

His father's voice began to shake. "James, we would be bad parents if we just let it go."

All three were crying a little, looking down and trying to hold back tears.

"You can go now," his father said before getting up and leaving the room.

James went up to his room and cried for a long time. He was glad it was over. He felt a little bit guilty for lying to his parents, but he didn't trust them enough to tell them about finding Zintar. He was exhausted from the long day, and it didn't take long for him to drift off to sleep.

The Old Inn

A few days later, James was sitting up in his room, playing with some of his toys. His mother came in and said, "James, your father and I are going for a walk. Would you like to come with us? I know it's not the same as playing in the forest, but it would be good for you to get outside and have some fresh air."

James was rather bored, so he decided to join them. There wasn't a lot going on in the quaint village. The sun was barely peeking through the clouds, and the wind came through in gusts that nearly blew David's hat off. They began walking closer to the old inn, and James wondered whether he might catch a glimpse of Zintar. He was a little worried because he hadn't heard from Mrs. DuCrét or Saleem about whether Zintar was okay. James assumed he would have heard something if not, though.

When they arrived at the inn, Saleem was outside, tending to his gardens. He glanced up, smiled, and waved at them.

"Saleem!" David said as they walked over to the garden. "Your gardens still look great despite this dreadful weather."

Bella said hello, and James stood behind his parents and waved shyly.

"How's the new house treating you?" Saleem asked politely.

"Oh, it's coming along." David's voice drifted into a longwinded explanation of all the work they'd been doing on the house.

James's attention had shifted to the top floor of the inn. He hoped to see Zintar up there with Mrs. DuCrét. He could faintly hear the creak of the old rocking chair. He wanted to go up so badly, but it would be hard to sneak away.

"James"—Saleem's voice caught him off guard—"how would you like some chocolate from Switzerland? I had some travelers through the other day, and they left some."

James smiled.

Saleem winked at him, and he knew there was more to the comment than chocolate. "Why don't you run inside and grab a bar for your family? I'm going to show them a few more things out back here. It's in the cupboard on the second floor at the end of the hall. Do you remember where that is?"

"Yes, sir," James said with a huge smile. He ran for the entrance, and Saleem took David and Bella out to the rear of the inn. Saleem quickly glanced up at Rionzi DuCrét, who was peeking over the railing to see what the commotion was, and discreetly gave her a wink.

James approached the afterthought door at the end of the hall on the second floor. It felt just like the first time. He checked behind himself to make sure no one was watching and then quietly pushed it open. The door itself made a creaking noise that seemed to echo loudly throughout the empty halls. Trying to get that door to open quietly had always been a challenge. He wanted to run up the stairs as fast as he could and find his friend Zintar, but for some reason he couldn't. The stairs seemed to hold him at a slow pace and force him to wait in anticipation. He crept up the squeaky stairs. His eyes were fixed on the opening at the top. When he reached it, he scanned the room and caught sight of Mrs. DuCrét out on the balcony, drinking her coffee in the worn old rocking chair. He remembered the first time he had come up these stairs, when the same scene had lain before him. The memories made him smile.

As he stood in the middle of the room, lost in memory, he was suddenly tackled to the ground by his short mushroom-footed friend.

Rionzi DuCrét turned around and peered through the balcony doors at the tangled mess of boy and Fidori rolling around on the ground, laughing. They looked so happy together.

Rionzi and Zintar had enjoyed each other's

company over the past few days. They had talked a lot about their time on top of the trees together, and Zintar had even taken it upon himself to care for the plants in her apartment, which were in quite a sad state. But he was becoming a bit restless and lonely. She had seen him staring out into the forest with longing.

"Mrs. DuCrét, I'm not even sure I remember what home is anymore. It's been so long," Zintar had told her.

It had broken her heart to hear him say that. She had dreamed for so many years of being back with the Fidoris, and the memories had tortured

her lonely existence—yet here was a Fidori who had almost forgotten what such a beautiful place was like. The agony of missing home had nearly become unbearable for him.

Zintar had wondered whether James would be back to see him, and Rionzi DuCrét just hadn't known. When he hadn't come for a few days, she'd begun to worry. Zintar couldn't stay with her for long, but they hadn't even begun to work out a plan to take him home. How were they going to sneak him back out of Nemesté? And if they did succeed, how were they going to get back through the forest and into the darkest part of the woods without Simputus interrupting them? No doubt she was already devising an evil scheme, knowing they would try to return Zintar to his home. On top of it all, they weren't even sure where to go. The sight of James and Zintar playing together seemed to put all those worries out of mind for now.

Rionzi heard Saleem finishing up his garden tour with David's parents as they came around the front of the building. "James, you'd best be off," she said into the room where James and Zintar were just rising from the surprise attack. "Your parents will be looking for you soon."

James looked up at Mrs. DuCrét with worry. "Mrs. DuCrét, what're we going to do? How are we going to get Zintar home?"

The question had never been far from her mind. "I'm not sure, James, but you must go for now. We'll think of something." She said those words even though she wasn't entirely sure she believed them herself.

James stood up and quickly gave Zintar another hug. "I'll be back, buddy," he assured the lost-looking Fidori.

"James, don't forget the chocolate!" Rionzi reminded him as he ran down the stairs.

"Oh, right!" He had completely forgotten about it, but he found the chocolate in the cupboard Saleem had said it would be in.

"James, did you find it?" Saleem yelled up the stairs.

"Yes, coming!" James yelled back as he closed the cupboard door and ran down the hall.

Trouble Stirring

weary shadow crept into Nemesté that night. Simputus was growing impatient while waiting for the humans to return the Fidori to her. It had been nearly four days since his escape, and he hadn't even attempted to leave the inn. She decided she would stir things up a little in town.

She crept into the Roedeses' house as they slept. The Roedeses were an outspoken family with a lot of influence in the small village. They were the family who had wanted Rionzi DuCrét banished forever from Nemesté because of her wild stories. Ever since Saleem's father had taken to caring for the crazy old woman, they had done their best to make life miserable at the inn. They had tried to get it shut down, saying the building was unsafe—this was resolved when Saleem's father put a lock on the afterthought door—and had attempted to spread various lies about Saleem and the inn. None of it ever produced much fruit, but they tried nonetheless.

This was precisely the reason Simputus chose to visit their house. The Roedeses were very superstitious, and a vivid dream of Fidoris and Rionzi DuCrét would be just the thing to stir trouble up again.

When Simputus snuck out the open window after casting her spell, a loud scream could be heard from inside the Roedeses' house. Mr. Don Roedes woke up out of a nightmare, and the sudden scream of his wife startled him.

"Don, Don, are you awake?" Jane yelled as she leaned over and shook him.

"Yes, yes, Jane, I am," he replied.

"Oh, I've had the most awful dream." She began to cry.

Don sat up and flicked on the little pink lamp beside the bed. Nightmares always seem to drift away when the light is on. "There, there, dear," he said as he reached for her hand. "I had a pretty weird dream myself. What was yours about?"

"Rionzi DuCrét," Jane said with venom in her voice. "I looked out our kitchen window, and there were strange purple flowers marking a path down the street. They looked exactly like the ones Rionzi DuCrét claimed killed her husband. They had bright purple petals and a dark green stem, and an eerie black centre held the petals tight. The flower itself was creepy enough."

"I had those flowers in my dream, as well," Don said. "What else?"

"Well, as I followed the line of flowers with my eyes, I saw Rionzi DuCrét—except she had big mushroom feet, like those wretched creatures she spoke of. And she had Saleem. She had tied his hands and was dragging him along into the forest path. There was someone else being dragged along with them, too. It was a child from the village. I couldn't quite see who he was. The sky was green and purple with thick, thick clouds. Oh, Don, it was just awful."

"I know, I know. Mine wasn't quite the same. In mine, Rionzi DuCrét was just dancing in a field of those purple flowers, screaming a bloodcurdling scream," Don said.

"Oh, Don," Jane said, her whiney voice ringing. "What does it mean? She's going to kill us in our sleep, I know it. Why doesn't she die already?"

"There, there." He tried to comfort her with a soft voice, but comforting in times of need had never been a strength for Don. "Calm down. It was just a bad dream."

"It wasn't just a bad dream, Don! Don't you think it's a bit odd that we both had dreams about Rionzi DuCrét and woke up at the exact same time? When we walked by the inn the other day, I could feel her crazy eyes staring at us through the window. She probably put a curse on us!"

"A curse?" Don tried not to laugh, but Jane heard the mocking in his voice.

"Don't laugh at me. She's crazy, Don. I mean, how old is she? She shouldn't be alive. We've got to do something."

"Jane, listen to yourself. We failed once trying to run her out of town, and we had a much stronger case than a dream and a supposed curse."

There was a pause in the conversation.

"But it couldn't hurt to stir things up a bit," Don finally said. "We could check up on the old inn to make sure the cuckoo and the cuckoo keeper are following the law."

So, later that day, the Roedeses decided to pay Saleem a visit at the inn.

Saleem was up on the third floor, just inside the door that led out to the balcony. Since the return of the Fidori, Saleem had been spending a bit more time upstairs. Rionzi was commenting on how lovely it was to watch James and Zintar playing together when Saleem spotted the Roedeses making their way up the road.

"Oh, great," he said. "What do they want now?" The only reason the Roedeses ever came to that end of town was to cause trouble for Saleem.

Rionzi turned and saw them coming, as well. "We should hide Zintar."

"I know. They likely won't come up here, but just in case. Where should we put him?" Saleem said.

"I know this sounds crazy, but do you have any guests on the second floor?" Rionzi inquired.

"No." Saleem knew what she was thinking. "We could put him in a closet in one of the rooms down there. They would never think to look there."

"I just don't trust them not to come up," Rionzi said.

"Yes, it will have to do," Saleem agreed. He walked into the apartment and called for Zintar, then briefly explained what was going on. Although Zintar was afraid, he agreed to hide in the closet.

Saleem grabbed his branchy hand gently and walked him down to the second floor. Before exiting the apartment, they scanned the corridor to make sure it was empty. Saleem latched the door with a padlock that he only ever used when the Roedeses came to visit. Then they made their way to the first room they came upon. The closet was dark and musty.

"Well, I'd best go greet our guests," Saleem said. He looked into the scared Fidori's eyes. "It's only for a little bit, Zintar. I'm so sorry that we have to do this. People can be cruel, and I don't want you hurt."

Zintar's big blue eyes stared at him in confusion. It was very hard for a Fidori to imagine such cruelty, but being with Simputus for so long had given him some idea of it. "When can I go home?"

"Soon, I hope." At that moment, Saleem realized the urgency of getting Zintar back to his people. Though he was among friends here, he was scared, confused, lost, and lonely. They could not keep him trapped much longer or the inn would turn into the dark cave of Simputus. They couldn't do that to a creature they loved. Saleem pondered these things as he closed the door on Zintar and made his way to greet the Roedeses.

They opened the door just as he reached the bottom of the stairs. "Well, this is a pleasant surprise," Saleem said. "Is there something I can do for you?"

"Don't be smart with us," Don shot back. "You're up to something suspicious here. We can feel it."

For a brief moment of panic, Saleem worried they had found out. "You can feel it?" he said.

"There's a foul smell in the air," Don said, "and your face has lies written all over it." They both glared at Saleem as if to make him confess.

Saleem pretended he was confused. "Look, I have no idea what you're talking about." He hoped they didn't hear the tremble in his voice.

"Is the old hag still around?" Don hoped his disrespect for Rionzi DuCrét would anger the innkeeper. "I mean, she hasn't died yet, has she?"

"Yes, she's still alive and in quite good health, I might add, considering her age," Saleem replied.

"That's a shame. As her guardian, I assume you know where she is," Don said with a scowl.

Saleem didn't like it when people talked about Rionzi as if she were a dangerous animal that might escape. "Yes, Don, I know what I'm supposed to do. I am a second-generation caregiver for Mrs. DuCrét."

"You speak of her as if she's an important person. *Mrs. DuCrét,*" he said. "She's a crazy lunatic, and I'm not sure why she's still living or why she must haunt our streets." Don was getting riled up.

Saleem hated the way Don insulted Rionzi, but at the same time he couldn't act too personal towards her. If he did, the Roedeses' suspicions would only grow, and at this time he didn't want too much suspicion around the inn. "Don, look, she's a person, and, though a bit crazy, she has a name that I'll continue to use. Is there something else you wanted to say?"

Jane answered this time. "We were just popping in to make sure all the rules of her living here were being kept. It's good to keep on top of these things with a surprise visit every now and again."

"Plus," Don chimed in, "we just enjoy your company."

"Well, that is kind, Don. Would you care to stay for a cup of tea?" The comment from Saleem was more of a challenge than an invitation.

Don played along. "Ha, wouldn't we all love that? Look, Saleem, we just want to have a look around. Can you please come with us to guard us from her craziness?"

"Honestly, Don, what do you think she's going to do? She's one hundred and fifty years old," Saleem said. "Where would you like to go first? Did you want to go up and say hi to her? I'm sure she would love the company."

"No, no, that won't be necessary," Jane said with a hint of fear in her voice.

Don continued. "Saleem, we would like to make sure the lock is still functioning. We would also like to see the biweekly walk log. We worry you might be letting her out a bit more than she should be."

"Right, and I would record it, too," Saleem said.

"Don't joke like this, Saleem. I'm warning you," Don said.

Saleem walked over to the front desk, where the keys were stored, and picked up the one for the upper apartment. "All right, let's go."

They wandered up two flights of stairs to the afterthought door at the end of the hall. Saleem thought about making some joke about being careful as he opened the door, but he decided against it. The old lock echoed as the key opened it up. "I'll be a minute, but you'll hear her voice," he said.

This ritual had been performed a few times. The Roedeses would wait at the bottom of the stairs, Saleem would walk up and talk to Rionzi, asking her some question just so they could hear her voice, and then he would come back down. Just knowing she was up there usually calmed them down a little.

Saleem decided to do things a bit differently this time. "Hello, Mrs. DuCrét," he said loud and clear as he walked up the stairs. "There are some guests who would like you to say hi to them." He caught Rionzi's eye and winked.

"Leave me be in my sorrow. Leave me be!" she said loudly, sounding angry, but she smiled at Saleem.

Saleem walked back down the stairs to a surprised and slightly scared Don and Jane. As Saleem closed the door and began locking it, Don put his hand firmly on his shoulder and said in a threatening tone, right into his ear, "We'll find what you're hiding."

Saleem said nothing and began walking back down the hallway. Jane was right on his heels, obviously afraid of being left alone with the old lady, but Don sauntered slowly and peered into the room Zintar was hiding in.

"There's a lot of empty space up here today." Don took a few steps into the room.

Saleem tried not to look nervous, but he quickly went into the room, as he knew a scared Fidori was hiding in the dark closet.

"Do you think the old lady ever comes down and uses all this empty space?" Don said. "It would be hard to know if she did in such a big building."

"But I lock the door so she cannot." Saleem was beginning to sweat. He couldn't even imagine what would happen if Don opened the closet and saw the creature standing there.

"Yes. Still, she may have another way down. An old building like this is likely to have a few secret passages. Maybe we need to see a blueprint or something," Don said as he inched closer to the closet door. He reached out and put his hand on the handle, slowly wrapping his fingers around the knob.

He seemed to be watching Saleem, seeing if there was any hint that he might be lying about something. Saleem could feel a bead of sweat trickle down his back. What was he going to do?

An Unexpected Phone Call

"Don, come now," Jane said, poking her head into the room. "There's nothing here. Let's go look at the log book and be away from this place. I hate being so close to her."

Don looked at Saleem one last time, and Saleem simply turned around and walked out the door.

After a few steps down the hallway, he heard the sound of Don and Jane following him. He slowly and quietly let out the breath he had been holding. When they reached the front desk, Saleem pulled out the log book.

Nothing much was said afterward, but as the Roedeses walked out the door after examining the book, Don turned around and said, "We might come by again unexpectedly."

Saleem was happy to see the door close behind them. Just as he stood there, wondering what had caused the Roedeses to be so suspicious, the phone rang.

"Hello, Nemesté Inn, how can I help you?"

"Ah, yes, Saleem. It's David."

"Oh, yes, what can I do for you?" Had the Roedeses already begun spreading rumors?

"Well, I have a question for you. Bella and I need to go away for a week, and we can't take James with us. Normally we would ask Bella's mother to watch him, but she's quite ill these days and wouldn't be able to do it. I know you're busy and such, but would you be willing to watch James next week for us? He would be in school all day, and he could help out around the inn in the evenings if you'd like. He's a very good worker."

Saleem couldn't have imagined a better phone call.

David continued. "We'll pay you, of course. It's just that James really liked it there, and it might be good for him to have a bit of space to run around in—preferably not in the forest."

David sounded like he would continue to try to convince Saleem of his proposition, but Saleem cut him off. "David, it would be fine for him to stay here at the inn." David couldn't see it, but Saleem's smile covered his entire face as he answered. "Yes, it might be good to have some life around here."

David sounded just as happy. "Oh, well, that's great. I think he would really enjoy that, but you make sure to put him to work in the evenings for a bit. Mind you, he'll have some homework, but he should have time to help you out."

"Oh, yes, of course," said Saleem, knowing full well what kind of work they would be doing.

A few more logistics were discussed, and it was settled. James would arrive on Saturday and stay through until Thursday. Saleem thought they might even be able to get Zintar home over the weekend, and James would be back in school on Monday without a question asked. He hung up the phone and ran as fast as he could up the three flights of stairs.

As soon as he passed through the afterthought door, he yelled for Rionzi.

She waddled in from the balcony. "Good grief, Saleem. Do you want all of Nemesté to hear you calling for me?"

He immediately stopped and smiled at her.

She couldn't quite guess what he was so stupidly excited about. "Surely the visit with the Roedeses was not that exciting."

In all the excitement, he had nearly forgotten about them. "Oh, right, yes. That was terrible."

Rionzi was getting a little impatient with his silly smile. "Well, boy, spit it out. What has possessed you to wake the village with my name?"

"Yes, sorry. James is coming to stay with us for a week!" he said, his smile growing even wider.

Rionzi still only knew about the Roedeses' visit and was very confused. "Are the Roedeses going to lock him away forever, too? Did he say something?"

Saleem was still grinning. "No." He took a deep breath and explained.

Rionzi completely understood Saleem's excitement, though she hid it a little better. She stared right into his wide open eyes, smiled a little, and said, "We can take him home, Saleem. We can take him home."

Saleem couldn't help himself. He walked over and gave Rionzi a hug.

She was a little surprised, but she welcomed it. They both started laughing a little.

His face turned more serious. "Now, about the Roedeses." There was a brief pause. "They're very suspicious that you're haunting the streets at night. Where would they get such an idea?"

Rionzi knew. She had felt it ever since they had been home—only brief moments, but unmistakable feelings of fear. There were times throughout the day and night when she could feel that dreaded gaze upon her. She tried to ignore it, but Simputus's gaze was hard to forget. A minute later, it would be gone. It was as if she was staring from some faraway hill, studying, scheming, and fuming. Last night, Rionzi had also had a terrible nightmare, and she knew the wretched creature was not far away.

"Saleem," she said, "Simputus is behind this, you know. She has been watching us. I can feel it, and I have a sneaking suspicion she may have paid a visit to the Roedeses to cause trouble. If we can just keep them away for a few more days, we can take Zintar home."

"Zintar!" Saleem said out loud. He suddenly realized they had forgotten him down in the closet. Their forgetfulness made them laugh and, for the time being, eased their worry about Simputus.

James could barely contain his excitement when his dad told him the news. An entire week at the inn! He couldn't believe his luck.

"Will that be okay?" Bella asked in a tone that suggested she was worried about the arrangements.

"Oh, yes, Mom, that'll be okay. Saleem is a nice man," he said, trying not to show too much excitement. "Maybe he'll have more chocolate for me."

Bella and David hadn't expected James to take the news so well. He didn't usually like being sent off to a stranger's place, but perhaps because he had been there before, he was okay with it.

The rumors in town about Rionzi DuCrét had increased, as the Roedeses had made a few phone calls and home visits to stir things up a little.

"Do you think we have anything to worry about?" Bella asked David when James was out of earshot.

"No, I don't think so," David answered. "The Roedeses have always exaggerated when it comes to matters of Rionzi DuCrét. They treat Saleem as if he's a criminal for taking care of the old woman. I don't deny that she's a bit strange or that it's a bit weird that she's still living, but I don't think she's any great danger to the village, especially at her age. And besides, Saleem has her all locked up. He has ever since his father died, and there's never been an incident."

"Until now!" Bella interrupted.

"A dream, Bella. Yes, it's a bit weird that they

both had a scary dream, but it's no reason to believe she's going to do something," David said with a bit of annoyance. "James will be fine."

David had a way of arguing for whatever he wanted at that moment, even if it changed from one day to the next. Had he not been so set on James staying at the inn with Saleem, he would have likely been arguing that the Roedeses were on to something and demanded further investigation. But he had other plans that were more important than an investigation into Rionzi DuCrét.

The day finally came when James could go to the inn. His mom helped him pack all he would need for the week, and when she left to finish her own packing, James snuck a few other items in his bag that he thought might be useful for returning Zintar to his home.

James found within himself a mixture of emotions. Returning Zintar meant he might never see him again. This made him sad. But he was also excited for the adventure through the forest and a climb to the top of the trees, where Zintar said he would be able to see forever. He was also a bit scared because he knew Simputus was lurking around. He, too, had felt her presence in the village for a few nights. He wished she would just go away and leave them alone. However, these thoughts and worries were shrinking in his mind, as he knew that tonight he would be in the inn, safe from harm with his friend.

"James, time to go!" his dad yelled up the stairs.

When they arrived, Saleem came to greet them as they stepped out of the car.

"Saleem, thank you again for doing this for us. We're so grateful," David said as he gave a solid handshake to the innkeeper.

"Oh, it's not a problem at all." Saleem smiled at James as he said it.

"You've got the old lady under control?" David asked. "The Roedeses were a bit concerned. They say there have been strange happenings lately in the village. Is there any truth to it?"

"Well, if you're calling their dreams 'strange happenings,' then I suppose there have been some, but I don't know how they connect these dreams with a hundred-and-fifty-year-old lady." Saleem was a bit annoyed at the accusations, but he tried not to show it. "I know the task that has been handed down to me, and I don't take it lightly. Mrs. DuCrét is well looked after and well secured."

"That's good. I was just checking." David was satisfied with the answer and eager to get going. "Well, Bella, my dear, should we be off?"

They gave James a hug and a kiss, then got into the car and drove off. James patiently stood

outside with Saleem and waved as his parents left, but he was secretly itching to go in and see Zintar.

When they were out of sight, the innkeeper turned to James and said, "You're just in time."

"In time for what?" James gave Saleem a puzzled look.

Saleem smiled and answered, "In time for our team meeting on the third floor."

When James arrived on the third floor, he looked around desperately, but he couldn't see Zintar anywhere. Mrs. DuCrét was in her usual place out on her balcony, rocking in her rocking chair. "Hi, Mrs. DuCrét," James said as he wandered out to the balcony. "Do you know where my friend is?"

"I think he went for a walk in the town," she said with a grin.

"No he didn't!" Just as James said that, he heard a snicker from behind the couch. He turned quickly and ran over. "There you are."

Zintar stepped out from behind the couch and smiled.

"All right, guys, we need to talk," Saleem interrupted. He had other chores to attend to and wanted to discuss the plans for getting the Fidori home. Mrs. DuCrét slowly made her way inside the apartment and joined the others in her dingy living room.

Saleem began. "What day should we set out?"

"Tonight, without a doubt!" Mrs. DuCrét said, a bit harsher than she'd meant to. Of course they had to set out tonight—what kind of a question was that? She was a bit out of sorts because she had been worrying day and night over the journey back to the treetops. It had been so long, and she had never properly said goodbye. She had simply set out one day because she couldn't live with the guilt she felt when she believed she had killed Zintar. Now she felt guilty for vanishing instead of letting the others know. Despite her fears and worries, though, she had to help Zintar get back. They'd had such a lovely time together this past week, telling stories and remembering what it was like above the trees.

She had confessed to Zintar how she left, and she could tell he was saddened by it. Fidoris didn't understand guilt and shame very well because they rarely had need of it, but he assured her that though the Fidoris might not understand, they would accept her back. They didn't hold grudges well, either, especially with friends.

Saleem's voice broke into her thoughts. "Yes, of course we should leave tonight. Where do we go?"

James knew the forest best of all, and he knew mostly where they needed to go. He knew how to get them to the beginning of the darkest part of the forest. He had been near it a few times, and he was fairly certain, after hearing Mrs. DuCrét's story, that that was where she had climbed the tall tree to escape Simputus and had found the Fidoris. "I know how to get us to the darkest part of the forest," he said. "I think if we go far enough in there, we can just climb a tree to the top."

It seemed easy enough, but deep down they all knew it would not be so. Strange things lurked in those parts of the forest—though their biggest problem would likely be Simputus, and she was becoming less of a stranger to them. She was scary enough in the light, but fears are always exaggerated in the dark.

"What are we going to do about Simputus?" Saleem asked the question they were all thinking.

"What can we do?" Rionzi said with fear and determination. "She will be with us the whole time, I'm sure. She's watching. She knows James is here now. She has been with us since we returned. We'll need to be on our guard."

"I brought the sap," James piped in. "That'll help."

"We'll have to stay with each other the whole time," Zintar added. "She only bothers us atop the trees if we're alone. It's harder to scare people when they're together."

"Well, you all should get some rest," Saleem suggested. "I've got work to do to prepare for my absence tomorrow. Let's leave tonight at midnight."

"And hope she doesn't see us," Rionzi added as she stared out the window.

A Night in the Forest

Four black spots emerged from the door of the old inn. From where Simputus was sitting on the edge of the forest, that was what the four companions looked like. She had been watching the inn for nearly a week now, waiting for this moment. She had paid the Roedeses another visit, hoping to wake them in the night so they would catch a glimpse of Rionzi DuCrét, but the group of four had decided to take a different route around the village and not pass by their house. She smiled a little because she knew it meant they feared her, and instilling fear in people brought her the only type of joy she had ever experienced. Now, though, it wasn't very joyful at all. In fact, it was more of a brief satisfaction in knowing she held power over someone. But it never lasted long and always left her feeling lonelier than before.

When Nemesté was built, all the purple flowers had been destroyed—and along with them all the keepers of the flowers. Somehow, Simputus had survived the massacre and was the only remaining keeper. She had managed to keep one single seed, which she'd planted in this very spot. The flower wasn't always harmful to humans, but when she planted this seed, she had discovered that the poisonous hatred she held for the village people seeped into the flower as it grew, and a new species was created. After this discovery of the capacity of her hate, she realized she could also influence people's emotions, and this gave her a great sense of power that grew into an addiction, making her feel good one minute, then lousy the next. The strange thing about addictions is that you keep coming back for the good feelings.

Still feeling good about the power of fear, Simputus watched the party head into the forest.

They all felt her gaze strongly as the trees seemed to close around them. James grabbed Zintar's hand and didn't let go. They hoped to reach the entrance to the darkest part of the forest within a few hours, provided they didn't get lost. The moon was bright, which was risky in the village but helpful in the forest.

"What are your fears tonight?" Zintar suddenly said. The other three companions had been lost in thought, battling their fears alone. They hadn't thought talking about them would be any good, but the warmth that seemed to fill each of them as Zintar asked the question made them realize that perhaps talking about fears might not be such a silly idea. At first, the noise of talking seemed unwise, but Simputus was following them anyway, so what would it matter if they talked?

Zintar noticed the hesitation in his friends and decided to begin by sharing his fears, hoping it would encourage them. "My greatest fear is that we will reach the top of the trees and…" He paused a moment. He wasn't sure he could say it out loud anymore.

James noticed his hand twitching a little and squeezed it tight to reassure him it was okay. "And what?" James prompted.

Zintar took a breath. "And they won't be there. That all we've been talking about is just made-up stories of a land far away that doesn't really exist."

"Zintar," James began, "I felt that way after I moved to the city and Mom and Dad told me you weren't real, just imaginary. I began to believe that maybe they were right, but something inside me must have still believed, because when I came back to Nemesté, I still kept searching even if I wasn't sure. I guess I was searching because of hope."

After a small pause, Rionzi DuCrét spoke. "Zintar, I, too, have felt that way. When the people of Nemesté told me I was crazy for believing that such creatures as Fidoris existed, I spent many lonely days wondering whether you were real. I was so torn, because if Fidoris did exist, it meant I had played a part in killing you, but if you didn't exist, it meant I was crazy. But, as James said, hope kept me searching."

Saleem took a turn sharing his fears, as well. "I believed the stories of the crazy Rionzi DuCrét as soon as my father, who also believed, told them to me. I could never share this with anyone, though, so at times I wondered whether I was right to believe such nonsense. But, other than believing in a creature that was a bit strange, there was no reason Rionzi couldn't be trusted. In fact, if anything, her age and the fact that she had never once denied the existence of the Fidoris were more proof that they did exist."

The fear within Zintar lessened as his friends shared their own doubts with him. It didn't quite disappear, but it was comforting to know he was not alone. They began sharing other fears. Rionzi DuCrét shared how she feared King Motumbu would not forgive her for what she had done. James shared his fears of leaving the Fidoris, assuming they found them, and returning to Nemesté to continue on with his life in a world full of people who would never believe his best friend existed. Saleem shared fears about what would happen to Rionzi DuCrét if she outlived him, which it sometimes seemed she might.

By the time they had all shared their fears and laughed a little about them, they realized they were at the entrance to the darkest part of the forest. It was like a wall of blackness even darker than the night. None had ever ventured this close before. The moon, which had been lighting their way through the forest, could not seem to break through the thick canopy that lined the top of the darkest part. They knew this was the path they had to take, but they decided to wait until morning. The forest would be dark in the daylight, but they would at least be able to see a little, and with Simputus so close, they thought it would be better to venture under the thick canopy when it wasn't so dark.

Again, since Simputus was likely already aware of their whereabouts, they decided to build a small campfire to take the chill of the night away. They planned to rest for a few hours, and then, when the sun was bright in the sky, they would venture into the darkest part of the forest together.

Simputus watched as they all slowly faded into sleep around the glowing fire. She had hoped to sneak in and snatch the Fidori, but the four travelers had fallen asleep tangled up with one another. Removing any one of them wouldn't be possible without waking the rest. She decided she would plan an attack when they ventured into the dark. If she could somehow separate them, it would be easier to snatch the Fidori back. She wasn't sure why she wanted him so badly. She didn't want to harm him or use him for anything. She simply enjoyed having complete control over him. Fidoris were different than humans and were harder to scare. Part of it was that they were always together, but these creatures had a sap that killed her flowers, and unlike the pathetic humans, they had magic, as well.

With the people she tried to scare, she only held a temporary power over them, because something else would inevitably capture their attention, and soon the fear would be pushed aside and forgotten for a time. It irritated Simputus that they forgot her. When she took Zintar in, she had realized that he could not be so easily distracted. She thought perhaps she could capture all four companions and have them completely under her power. The thought was almost too overwhelming.

While the group slept, she decided to leave them a little reminder that she was not far away. She planted a circle of purple flowers around them so they would remember. The deep black middles stared at them as they slept. She had no doubt their dreams would soon turn to nightmares. With that evil thought, she disappeared into the blackness.

~

James woke up sweating and screaming. The others were soon awake and happy to be so, since they, too, had been dreaming terrible things.

Rionzi DuCrét was the first to notice the circle of flowers. "She's been here. Don't move too quickly! We're surrounded by flowers," she warned.

The sun was beginning to rise, and a dull grey lit up the forest. They had made it through the night with only a few nightmares and a circle of purple flowers around them. Simputus hadn't attempted any attack but seemed to have set out a warning. That worried them a little, but they chose to keep positive and focus on the fact that they had made it through the night.

Saleem had packed a little food for breakfast: some rolls, butter, jam, and a little coffee for himself and Mrs. DuCrét. As Saleem prepared the rolls, James used the tiniest amount of sap to kill a few flowers so they could safely get out of the circle. He didn't want to use too much, because he worried they might need it later.

"She'll try to split us up," Rionzi said as she finished her jam roll. "James, don't lose Zintar. We'll all do our best to stick together, but I think she's mostly after him. Once we're far enough in, just pick the largest tree and climb it. Don't look down—keep climbing, and climb fast. Once you're near the top, the branches become a lot closer together, and you can walk along to different trees. Try to find the beamers." She looked at Zintar and smiled. "From up top, they look like nasty, scary holes, but from down below they're bright and cheerful. If you can find one, climb up there, because you'll save yourself a lot of scratches and energy. If you have to, you can climb through the canopy, although I wouldn't choose that option first. If we get separated, whoever is with Zintar will get him to the top. If you don't have him, linger and try to find the others, but don't linger too long."

The bags were packed, and they set off into the darkest part of the forest. Rionzi DuCrét had been here before, so she wasn't in shock, but the other three hadn't expected the darkness to be so heavy. The canopy was so dense above them that there was only a faint glow through the trees. They could see one another's outlines, but not much more. Terrible shrieks from birds echoed through the dark, giving them an uneasy feeling.

Saleem glanced over his shoulder and watched the light disappear beyond the trees. They were completely surrounded by darkness now. He felt a soft hand take hold of his and begin guiding him along. He kept staring back to where the light had once been, but it was no longer there.

The Dark Forest

he hand let go as gently as it had grabbed him. Saleem looked behind himself, expecting to see the others, but no one was in sight. He stopped dead in his tracks and turned in a circle. All he could see was darkness. Where had they gone? Who had been holding his hand? A shadow caught his eye not more than a few feet in front of him. He recognized it from when he had followed Rionzi DuCrét and James into the forest: a scraggly, beastly character. He'd also seen the thing in his dreams, and it was never a good sign.

For a brief moment, he thought that perhaps he'd fallen asleep and was in the middle of a horrid nightmare, but he couldn't wake up, and that thing was walking straight towards him. He turned to run, but his feet tripped over a large root, and he fell flat on the ground. When he looked up, he thought for a moment that he could see dust sparkling in a beam of light, but whatever it was disappeared, and Simputus's shadow crept over him. He froze in fear. He didn't know what was going to happen. Her black eyes stared right back into his. Saleem tried to look away, but some unnatural force compelled him to keep staring. He thought he might faint.

She pulled out something from behind herself and dropped it. It fell hard and landed right on his chest with a light thud. It was a purple flower. It felt odd on top of him. It didn't float down the way a flower normally would—it just dropped. It felt heavy, but from the inside, the way he sometimes felt deep down in his gut when he'd done something wrong and guilt and shame overtook him. He began to breathe heavily. He watched Simputus turn and walk away, leaving him. Saleem had heard the stories from both James and Rionzi about the deadly flowers. He realized with relief that they didn't seem to be affecting him as quickly as the others had said.

As he lay there in shock, he heard more footsteps coming through the forest.

"Saleem, Saleem!" It was the voice of Rionzi DuCrét. She nearly tripped over him, then gasped in horror at the sight of the flower. "Get up!" she cried out. "We've got to get you to the top!"

"It's not doing anything," he tried to explain.

"It's on top of your shirt, that's why," she snapped back. She grabbed his hand and began pulling him to his feet. The flower fell to the ground, but she could see its outline in the fabric. The shirt might have been enough to stop the spread of the poison, but she wasn't sure. "I'm afraid it'll seep through," she said. "You've got a bit more time, but not much. I don't know where we are, but we've got to start climbing. I've lost James and Zintar, and James has the sap. I knew she had gone after you. We can meet them at the top."

"I think there's a beamer near. I saw a light," he said.

"I hope so, because by the time we get up there, I'm not sure we'll have any strength left," Rionzi said.

"Ah!" Saleem yelled as he fell to the ground. "I can feel it now. I don't think I'm going to make it."

Rionzi knew that the flower was indeed deadly if not properly treated, but she also knew that it played games with people's minds, causing them to give up long before they physically needed to. "Saleem!" she said in a stern voice. "We need to climb now. Stand up and follow me."

Her tone surprised the innkeeper. He wasn't sure whether he was more afraid of dying out here on the dark forest floor or disobeying Rionzi's command. Somehow, the old lady's demand won, and he was on his feet, reaching for a branch above his head. He pulled himself up and then up again. He was afraid he might lose Rionzi, who had climbed ahead of him at a surprisingly fast pace.

The effects of the purple flower were beginning to weigh on him. He desperately wanted to give up and just allow himself to die. Each branch he reached for seemed wobbly. He was trying to follow, but things were spinning around him, and he wasn't sure which direction was up or down. He tried rubbing his eyes, hoping things would clear, but it didn't seem to help.

Just as he steadied himself on the trunk of a big tree, he started wondering if perhaps he should sit down a moment—but Rionzi's voice interrupted his hopeless thoughts.

"Saleem!" she yelled. "We're halfway there, and you're not dead yet. So keep climbing!" She knew it was rather harsh, but she couldn't allow him to stop. She couldn't carry him, and if she left him, he would die. She put out her hand, grabbed his, and propped him back up. She helped steady his quivering legs and stared him right in the eyes. She tried to look brave so Saleem could have some hope, but deep down she wasn't sure she had the strength to make it, either.

He got back on his feet and started climbing again. Rionzi was growing tired, but she couldn't slow down, not if they were going to make it to the top. A glimmer of hope came when she saw light shining through the canopy. Saleem had seen the beamer from down below, but when she looked behind her again, Rionzi realized the innkeeper couldn't go any further.

The Treetops

intar and James had somehow lost Rionzi DuCrét in the dark. They were both whispering her name, hoping she wasn't far, but to no avail. They were alone, and the darkness seemed to close in tight around them. They stood close, holding each other's hands, unsure of which direction to go. Suddenly, they felt fear so strong that they knew they had to begin to climb.

"But what if she's taken Mrs. DuCrét and Saleem?" Zintar asked, dreading even the thought of it.

"Mrs. DuCrét said to climb to the top of the trees if we got split up. They might already be up there. We have to go now," replied James, trying to be brave.

That was the end of the discussion, and they began their ascent. The tree they had chosen had a lot of branches close together, which made it easier to climb. About halfway up, James glanced back down, and he caught a glimpse of Simputus at the bottom of the tree. Even though it was too dark to see more than a shadow, somehow Simputus's rich dark colours glowed as James gazed upon her for the first time. He'd only ever seen her flowers before and had used his imagination to guess what she looked like from Rionzi DuCrét's stories—but that was nowhere near as frightening as staring into her black eyes, which stared back at him with such hatred.

As James stood there, frozen in fear, Zintar grabbed a hold of his shirt and began pulling him upwards. "Come on, James, she's coming!"

James knew that, but he couldn't take his eyes off her. Finally, he turned and began heading up the tree. He could probably have climbed faster, but Zintar was struggling. Suddenly, his big round feet slipped off the branch he was stepping on, and he came crashing into James. Luckily, James's footing was firm, and he caught his friend. In saving Zintar, though, he had dropped the sap, and it went crashing down, missing Simputus altogether. As the Fidori tried to climb again, using his hands to grip instead of his feet, James looked back and saw that Simputus was quickly gaining on them. How could she climb so fast?

Finally, when they neared the top of the trees, they realized that they were nowhere near a beamer. Above them was a thick canopy of leaves. They began digging their way through, but it was slow going. Thick sap started to coat them from all the branches they were breaking. That was a huge relief, despite the stickiness all over their bodies. They knew Simputus wouldn't dare follow them up into the sap if they could just get far away enough.

She was nearly at their heels, but they were nearly through. Zintar pulled himself up and ripped a few more branches off. James glanced nervously down as Simputus scrambled closer and closer.

"James, give me your hand!" shouted Zintar.

As Zintar pulled James up, Simputus grabbed his foot and began pulling down—but Zintar took one of the broken branches and threw it at her. The sap from it dripped on her, and she immediately let go, sending Zintar and James smashing through some more branches.

They were sticky, cut, bruised, and very tired, but they were almost there. They could see wide sunbeams, and it seemed they were out of danger now, as Simputus was out of sight. Finally, Zintar's hand sprang through the canopy to the blue sky. He ripped a few more branches, hardly able to believe they were nearly there. Finally, there was a space big enough for his head to fit through. With one last climbing effort, he heaved himself up. His big mushroom feet followed, and he was on top of the trees. He breathed in the fresh air and savoured the view of the lush green treetops meeting the brilliant blue sky. There really was a place like this. All he remembered about home really did exist. The Fidori nearly broke into tears, but he was distracted by James tugging at his feet, looking for something to grip and pull himself up.

"Zintar, help me up," James said.

Zintar pulled him up and smiled. "See? You really can see forever."

"We did it! We're here!" James said. He could hardly believe his eyes. "You were right. This is nothing like the field I tried to show you." He gave Zintar a big hug and knocked him down among the soft tops of the trees. They both lay there, soaking in the fresh air and the wind. Had they really made it? It seemed too good to be true.

"Somebody help me!" a voice called from a spot not too far away. "Somebody, anybody! Please, I need help."

Zintar and James realized it was Rionzi DuCrét crying desperately, and they ran towards her. Zintar had no problem with his big mushroom feet, bouncing along as fast as he could. James, on the other hand, found it very difficult to walk on top of the trees, and he stumbled rather slowly in the direction of the cries for help.

"Mrs. DuCrét, what's wrong?" Zintar said as he reached the beamer she was sticking out of.

"It's Saleem. He's just down there, but I need some sap. He's touched the flower and can't go any further," she puffed.

"Is Simputus down there?" Zintar asked.

"No, I haven't seen her. I've got to get some sap to him."

James finally made it to the beamer. "I'll go. It's safer. But I need some sap."

Zintar ripped off a fresh branch dripping with the sweet liquid. James grabbed it and, without a word, dropped below the tree. He came to Saleem, who looked unconscious, only a few branches down. He could see Mrs. DuCrét and Zintar staring through the beamer at him. Saleem was in bad shape. James hoped the sap would still work.

He touched the sticky end of the branch to Saleem's lips, and sap trickled into his mouth. Within seconds, he licked his lips, wanting more of the sweet lifesaving drink. The more he drank, the more he came alive. First, his eyes opened. Then he smiled. Then his arms moved, and then his legs and feet. Finally, he sat up and looked around.

"I thought I was a goner," he said.

"Can you stand?" James didn't want to rush coming to from a near-death experience, but they didn't have time for chitchat.

"I think so," Saleem said, trying to stand up on his wobbly legs.

"Simputus could be near. We need to get to the top," James said very seriously. He helped Saleem to his feet, and together they climbed.

"Wow" was all Saleem could say as he was pulled up by Mrs. DuCrét and Zintar. He stood up and stared into the distance.

The Reunion

hey've slept here recently," Zintar said. "There are fresh loose leaves around." He bent down and picked up little tiny branches and leaves. "See? These are the branches they scraped off this morning."

Rionzi smiled at the Fidori. She knew what he was talking about. James knew, as well, because he had heard Rionzi's story, but Saleem was confused. As they walked along—or, rather, stumbled along—Zintar explained to Saleem how the Fidoris grew into the trees at night, so each morning they had to wipe themselves off.

The four companions walked for about an hour to get well out of sight of the beamer. They feared Simputus might reappear. But they were very tired from their long walk and high climb to the treetops, and it was quite difficult for the humans to walk up there. They had to pick their steps carefully and, even so, often found themselves falling through the canopy.

"Can we rest, please?" James finally spoke up as he fell once more and scraped his leg a little.

"Maybe we should stop for the night," Rionzi agreed. She was just as tired, and it was getting on in the evening.

"I'll find some glow sticks," suggested Zintar, and he bounded off.

The others sat down and tried to watch the sunset, but within minutes they were fast asleep.

When Zintar returned, he set the glow sticks up around them and let his mind wander to being a Fidori again. He watched the big yellow sun fall beneath the trees. It almost looked like it had sunk right down into the centre of the canopy. And the rising of the moon was just as spectacular. It was big, and he could clearly see its face. The Fidoris had many stories about the man in the moon. Zintar wished one of his friends would wake up so he could share them, but they were exhausted, and they looked so content sleeping that he dared not wake them.

He lay back and started to shut his eyes when suddenly, out of the corner of his vision, just off to the right of the glowing moon, he saw a flicker of light. It was very far in the distance, but he saw it again. He rubbed his eyes. Perhaps it was the moon shimmering off something at the top of the trees—but as he kept looking at it, he grew more and more convinced that something was out there. Suddenly, he heard what sounded like laughter. It was hard to tell, though, because it was so far away. Could it really be the other Fidoris? It was almost too good to be true. He sat and listened for a little bit longer. Excitement grew inside him with every burst of laughter that reached his ears. He stood up and squinted again. It had to be the Fidoris.

Zintar began walking towards the light. He didn't even feel the tiredness anymore in his own body. He was too excited. With each step, he was more and more certain that it was the group of Fidoris. The glow was brighter, and the laughter was louder. It took him about half an hour to reach them. Finally, he was close enough that he could make out their faces. There was his family and friends, and King Motumbu and Queen Aliumbra, his dad and mom. He missed them so much, and here they were, standing only twenty feet away.

He couldn't hold back any longer. "Mom, Dad!" he yelled.

A surprised group of Fidoris around the glow stick campfire suddenly turned and looked at him. Zintar started with a brisk walk, but it turned into a run. Just as he reached them, he stopped face to face with King Motumbu and Queen Aliumbra. He smiled, and they smiled back. Motumbu reached down and pulled Zintar into a giant bear hug. Queen Aliumbra came over, as well, and soon the rest of the Fidori group joined.

It's hard to say how long this embrace lasted. Tears were shed and comments made about how unbelievable it all was, but after the moment was done, Zintar told them about his three friends, one of whom was Rionzi DuCrét. The Fidoris packed up their camp and decided to go nearer to the humans.

When they arrived, the three were still sound asleep, cozied into the treetops. The Fidoris decided not to wake them but settled themselves in for a night's sleep.

"Son," whispered Motumbu as they lay falling asleep, "tomorrow shall be a day of great story-telling."

The Fidoris

James was the first to wake in the morning. When he sat up and looked around, he couldn't believe his eyes. All around them was a pile of sleeping Fidoris. They looked so peaceful. He smiled. They had finally made it.

The morning was filled with laughter, introductions, and pleasant reunions. King Motumbu and Rionzi DuCrét sat together and talked.

"Rionzi, where did you go?" he asked. "One day you were here, and the next you were gone. You didn't even say goodbye."

"I know. It was wrong of me, and I'm sorry," she said. She had said that sentence so many times in her mind that it was hard to believe she was really saying it out loud.

"It was hard enough losing my son that day, but losing my human friend, too, was very sad. When I went looking and saw Simputus, she said he was dead and gone forever, and for some reason I believed her lies," Motumbu said.

"Sir," Rionzi began, trying to remember what she had imagined saying so many times before, "I saw her that day, too. I had gone looking for Zintar, as well. The night before, we had been talking about what was below the beamers, and I joked that someday he would have to come with me and see my village. He asked more about the beamers, and I said you could just climb down them. I forgot to tell him about the dangers that lay below the canopy.

"That morning, he was gone. I had a terrible feeling that maybe he had tried to climb down, so I went to the closest beamer. Simputus was sitting there beside it. I stupidly asked her if she had seen Zintar. She acted like she knew what I was talking about, but I'm not so sure she did, because I know for a fact that Zintar lived in the forest without her around for a long time. Anyway, I was angry, and I asked her what she had done with him. Oh, her smile made me cringe.

"'Yes, he was here,' she said to me. 'He wanted to know what was in the beamer, so I pushed him in so he could have a better view.' Then, before I could do anything, she jumped down the dark hole. I couldn't bear to face you again, thinking I had assisted in killing your son, but later I found out she was lying. Zintar had wandered down a beamer himself, but he had simply gotten lost in the forest. That was where he met James." Rionzi finally looked up and into Motumbu's deep, caring eyes. "Sir, that's the story, and that's why I left. I am sorry."

"Rionzi, dear friend," Motumbu said with much compassion in his voice, "I don't understand this shame and guilt you humans harbour so strongly that you fear you won't be accepted. With us, you will always be loved. It wasn't your fault, but even if it was, we forgive very easily."

"Thank you, sir." Rionzi burst into tears and stepped away from the group for a minute. She had been forgiven and was overwhelmed with joy at reuniting with her funny friends.

When she finally wandered back to the Fidoris, Zintar was in the middle of telling how he had met James that day in the forest. James broke in a few times to correct some exaggerations. They were quite a pair, Zintar and James.

As the day was getting on, Saleem and Rionzi realized the boy needed to go back at some point. During dinner, they talked to James and Zintar.

"James, have you thought about going home?" Rionzi said.

He looked at her with sad eyes. "Yes, I have, but I don't want to."

"Your family would miss you, and you would miss them," she said.

"I know," he replied. "But do we have to go so soon?"

"Yes, I'm afraid so," Saleem responded. "If we go tomorrow, I'll only have to explain one day of your absence from school. I think I can manage that." Saleem winked at him.

It made James smile. "Can I ever come back?"

Rionzi and Saleem smiled. "Oh, I imagine so," Saleem said.

"Are you staying here, Mrs. DuCrét?" James asked.

"Yes, I think I will. I've got nothing waiting for me back home except a village that would prefer I wasn't there—so you'll have to come see me again, too, James," Rionzi said.

The storytelling went far into the night. Motumbu told some classics, and Saleem even gave it a shot, though he clearly needed some practice.

Saying Goodbye

James opened his eyes just as the sun began waking up the world on top of the trees. The air was cool, but James was quite warm because he had slept right in the middle of a cluster of Fidoris. He watched the sky turn from dull grey to hazy pink.

"James," a familiar voice whispered, "are you awake?"

"Yes," he replied.

"Come with me." Zintar stood up and began carefully walking around all the sleeping Fidoris.

James followed behind, stumbling in the foliage. When they were out of earshot, they sat down. Sitting was much more enjoyable for humans on top of the trees.

"Do you really have to go today?" Zintar said with sadness.

"Mrs. DuCrét and Saleem said I have to."

The two friends sat like silhouettes on top of the trees, staring at the rising sun.

"Thank you, James, for helping me find my family." Zintar turned and looked at the others, who were just beginning to wake up. "And for being my friend when I was on the forest floor. Do you see now why I have these big feet?"

James laughed. The big mushroom feet had seemed so ridiculous on the ground, but up here they made so much sense. James looked down at his legs, which were covered in small scratches from trying to walk on the trees. He wished he had some big mushroom feet so he could bounce along and enjoy the springy treetops.

Saleem approached the two friends. They could tell it was him before even looking, because he was stumbling, not bouncing.

"Good morning, guys," he said. "James, I'm afraid we'll need to leave soon. We've got a long day ahead of us."

"Yes, I guess we do," replied James. He glanced back at the group. They were beginning to brush off the little branches that had grown into them overnight. James smiled as he watched the story Rionzi DuCrét had told him come to life. When his family moved back to Nemesté, he'd never imagined that he would be sitting on top of the trees with creatures nobody believed were real. He'd had a faint hope that he might find Zintar, but he hadn't imagined all of this.

Saleem put his arm around James, probably thinking the same thoughts. Here in front of them were the forbidden creatures of Nemesté.

"You will come and visit again, won't you?" King Motumbu said as James and Saleem packed and prepared to leave.

"Yes! As soon as we can," James replied. He looked up at Saleem, hoping he would agree. Then he caught the eye of Mrs. DuCrét. She looked happy here. The worn, concerned look she usually wore seemed to have disappeared. The worry lines were still there, permanently creased into her wrinkly skin, but there was a new glow and a new life in her. On her feet she wore makeshift shoes woven out of branches. They were wide enough so she didn't fall through the trees all the time.

Rionzi came up to James and wrapped her arms around him. "Thank you, my dear friend," she whispered in his ear. "I'll miss you, and I look forward to seeing you again."

Her breath still smelled of stale coffee, though James didn't mind so much, because it brought back such fond memories.

The group of creatures and one human with funny shoes gathered around the small beamer and watched as Saleem and James disappeared into the darkness below.

Neither of them had really thought much about the long walk back, but as the darkness surrounded them and the light from the beamer grew fainter and fainter, they remembered the dangers that lurked in the forest.

"Stay close, James. We mustn't get separated," Saleem said as he climbed behind the boy.

James had no intention of leaving Saleem behind. The fears they had nearly forgotten on top of the trees were now very present in the darkness. Their bodies were sore from the long climb up the other day, and each step down was painful, but they managed to reach the forest floor sooner than they'd thought they would. They both looked around the misty dark forest.

"Where do we go?" Saleem asked. He was completely disoriented. In the normal forest he was hopeless, but here in the darkest part he might as well have been walking around a strange planet with a blindfold on.

James took a few steps in one direction, trying to find something familiar to get his bearings, but he could find nothing. He wasn't exactly sure the best way out of there. "Let's try this way," he said, though he wasn't convinced it was right.

As they walked along, James could feel a burn in his calves, and he realized they were walking up a slight slope. It worried him a little because he knew they had walked a fairly flat trail on the way in. This felt like the right direction. He hoped it was just a different trail, though it wasn't really much of a trail at all. James could hear Saleem struggling a little with the incline. Finally, he saw a light up ahead, so he figured it had to be a clearing in the trees, and maybe he would be able to see where they were.

"I guess we can keep walking along this path," James said as they walked out of the dark forest. "See, there's the village." He pointed down the mountain and to the left. "I think it will meet up with a trail I sometimes walk on that goes up above Nemesté."

"Wow." Saleem was impressed. "It's amazing how well you know this forest. I've never ventured too far in."

They continued walking down the path as it wound back into some more trees. It was much brighter than before, and both were thankful to be out of the darkness.

"James, wait." Saleem spoke softly as he grabbed the boy's shirt to keep him from moving. "Look up ahead. There's a strange purple glow."

James stopped immediately. All of a sudden, a familiar fear came back. A flash of purple flowers flooded his mind, and he squeezed his eyes tight to try to make it disappear.

Together, they crept as quietly as they could towards the strange light.

"It's her," Saleem whispered, barely audible, as they caught sight of Simputus and a lone purple flower.

Simputus and Her Purple Flower

As quietly as they could, Saleem and James took a few steps back and crouched down behind the nearest bush. Simputus didn't seem to notice them.

The gangly creature was hunched over one of her poisonous flowers. She was sort of petting it and protecting it. It almost seemed to come to life and actually listen to her as she spoke to it.

"That creature reminded me of myself," she said, her eerie voice cracking.

"She's nothing like them," James whispered, a little too loudly, to Saleem.

Saleem covered the boy's mouth and gave him a panicked look.

Luckily, Simputus still hadn't noticed the pair spying on her. "Those Fidoris care for the trees the same way I care for you." She plucked a dead petal from the flower. "I only wanted him to be part of my family, the family those humans destroyed." She glared at the village below. "Is that so wrong?"

James and Saleem wondered what she was talking about. They felt a little sorry for her. She seemed sad and vulnerable and only wanted a family.

"But he left me!" The anger returned to her voice. "He left me and forgot all about me. Their power is too strong when they're together. I'll never get him back if he's up there. They have everything I had and everything I want. I hate them for it."

James couldn't be sure, but he thought he saw a tear roll down her face.

"Why me?" the creature continued. "Why my people? It's not fair, you know. I'll find a way to get him back, and I'll find a way to rid us of those humans." She stared at the village for a moment longer. Then she picked her flower, the snap echoing through the air, and she walked into the forest, thankfully on a different path than James and Saleem.

"Come, James." Saleem's voice was trembling. He dared not follow the path Simputus had taken. In fact, he thought it best to get off the path altogether.

James barely had time to get to his feet before the innkeeper was dragging him down the side of the mountain. It wasn't long before they both lost their footing on the steep slope and began sliding. James could feel rocks and sticks add scrapes to his legs. Saleem grabbed a tree to keep himself steady and then grabbed James by the shirt to stop his fall. It helped for a minute, and each of them took a deep breath. Then, all of a sudden, the tree broke and they were back to sliding, doing their best not to hit anything big. A scratch on the face from a swinging branch was better than face-planting into the side of a large tree.

After sliding for some time, they finally hit a flat spot and came to a crashing halt. When James looked up, he was happy to see they were almost in the village.

Saleem began to laugh a little.

"What's so funny?" James asked as he examined his injuries.

"I told your parents I'd look after you and you'd be safe with me." Saleem was still chuckling a little. He reached for a branch in James's hair. "I've done nothing but put you in danger since they left."

James had to smile a little, though he was still slightly annoyed at having been pulled down the mountain. He knew plenty of better ways to descend the steep hill.

They brushed themselves off, just like the Fidoris, and walked on a gentler slope down into Nemesté.

What Rionzi DuCrét Left Behind

The cool evening air descended on the village just as James and Saleem reached the inn.

"I'll make some dinner, James," the innkeeper said as he opened the door. James looked like his eyes were about to close right there in the foyer. "Then I suppose you ought to get some sleep. Tomorrow is Tuesday, and I've got to think of some excuse as to why you weren't at school today. Somehow I don't think 'sleepover with the Fidoris' will cut it."

James imagined the look his teacher would give him if Saleem did do that, and he thought it was funny, but he was too tired to respond. He hadn't realized how exhausted he was until they stepped inside the inn. James went upstairs to take a bath and change his clothes before dinner. Saleem had given him the room his family had stayed in when they were living at the inn.

Saleem got to work finding some food to make for dinner. Even though there were a few other guests at the inn that night, the big building felt empty. Rionzi DuCrét had been a part of this place, his home, since his childhood. They had rarely spoken throughout his life, but it had always been a comfort to have her upstairs, creaking away in her rocking chair. In a strange way, they had shared a lifetime together. He knew she was better off on top of the trees with the Fidoris and she would be happy living out her days there, but he already missed her.

James walked into the kitchen just as the microwave finished reheating some leftovers.

"I hope you like spaghetti." Saleem smiled as he brought over a steaming bowl of it.

"Oh, yes," James replied. "I'm starving."

"We didn't really have much to eat today, did

we? It's another thing to add to the list of not taking good care of you."

They both laughed.

As they ate dinner, James thought about the strange creature with the purple flower. "What do you suppose the purple flower lady meant when she said the humans destroyed her family?"

"I'm not sure," Saleem replied. "She seemed to say she took care of the purple flowers the way Fidoris take care of the trees. Maybe when Nemesté was built, her kind was destroyed." He thought for a minute longer. "I think, in a way, if that's what happened, it destroyed a part of her. But she's similar to the Fidoris."

"How is she like them? She's so mean and they're so caring," James said.

"Well, I don't know if she was always like that. Think about it, James. Both of these creatures seem to exist to be caregivers to a plant, and in some strange way it seems the plant is a part of them. Also, they have a weird magic that causes us to feel what they want us to feel."

James was nodding along, beginning to understand what Saleem was saying.

The innkeeper continued: "The Fidoris just wish us to feel warm feelings, and Simputus has been hurt, so she seems to want us to feel fear and pain, maybe as revenge."

It made sense, but James was having trouble concentrating. He was tired, and thoughts of Simputus still scared him.

Saleem seemed to notice. "Well, young man, you should go to bed."

"Yes, I think that's a good idea," James said. They went upstairs, and James crawled into bed.

"Goodnight, James," Saleem whispered as he closed the door. The poor exhausted boy was already sound asleep. He decided to walk up to Mrs. DuCrét's old apartment, the prison she had been kept in for so long. He smiled just thinking of her bouncing along with those funny creatures.

He wandered around the musty room on the third floor. It smelled of the old lady, which wasn't particularly pleasant, but the smell brought pleasant memories. He brushed his finger along the mantle, leaving a clear path through the thick layer of dust. He remembered watching his father help move her into the upper floor and telling him not to go up there. As a boy, he had often snuck to the front of the inn and hidden in a bush just to catch a glimpse of her on the balcony. His father had told him the stories of the Fidoris, but he hadn't ever been allowed to tell anyone.

As he scanned the tiny apartment, a bright beam of moonlight illuminated a piece of paper on the kitchen table. He picked it up and angled it into the light so he could read it. It was addressed to him.

"Dear Saleem, thank you for caring for me all these years. I am old, tired, and worn out. I think it's time I leave this town forever. I will not return this time, so you can tell the villagers they may rest peacefully at night knowing the crazy old lady is gone. Goodbye."

It was signed by Rionzi DuCrét. She had thought of everything. She must have known they would find the Fidoris and she would stay with them, and she had known he would need some evidence for the people of Nemesté that she was gone.

He looked out the window, over the town and at the sparkling lights of the cities in the valley below. He pictured the Fidoris sleeping on the treetops. He couldn't believe those creatures actually existed and that he was fortunate enough to have met them.

A Reflection

"What did the Roedeses want?" Bella asked as David walked back inside.

He had a troubled look on his face. "Rionzi DuCrét has left Nemesté."

"What?" She was shocked.

"Yes, apparently she left a note for Saleem saying she's left and will never return. Don is not convinced, even though he saw the note."

"Perhaps she's finally going to die, and she left the village to do so."

"Yes, maybe," he answered, not really paying attention. He went off into the kitchen to make some coffee.

Bella walked over to the window and watched James as he played outside. He seemed different.

He seemed happier than before. When they returned, she had asked him what he did while they were away.

James had answered, "Went to school and played outside." Then there had been a moment of hesitation, after which he had said that he and Saleem had gone for a walk in the forest and climbed some trees. As Bella retraced that conversation in her head, she suddenly realized that James had had a look, a glow, a reflection in his eyes when he said, "climbed some trees." Where had she seen that look before?

Suddenly, a memory resurfaced, a memory that had been buried so deeply she didn't know how it could come to mind: a memory of that day in the park in the shadow of the old church, when she was just a little girl. The old lady, Rionzi DuCrét, had had the exact same reflection in her eyes.

The END

Acknowledgements

First, I would like to thank my good friend Blake Allen. Together, we created the creatures called Fidoris while sitting on the "edge of the hedge" to prune the 15 foot high hedges in our village. I spent many evenings on the balcony of a Swiss chalet, reading each new installment of the story to him by candlelight. I could not have written this story without his imaginative contribution to the creation of the characters. Thank you to Destinée Media for publishing my first book. I am grateful to Ralph and Valerie for their willingness to invest in me as an author. A big thanks to Amanda Kramer Kaczynski for her amazing illustrations! She brought this story to life with her creativity/imagination. Thank you to Devon Brown for the cover design and to Julie Lundy for putting the interior together. There were many people who helped with editing this book. The first read through was done by my Aunt Lin who bravely took the first look. Val McCall from Destinée Media passed along suggestions that helped me as I considered the character development and general flow of the story. I would also like to thank Barb Falk for spending many hours reading through and editing a slightly better version of the story. Jeannie Blair was always there to answer questions, give me an honest opinion, and edit the small odds and ends that needed a sharper eye than mine. Thanks to Talia Leduc for doing the final cover-to-cover edit.

I would also like to thank Miss Blair's Grade 5 class, who became my first young audience to hear the book. They had great questions for me about being a writer and some thoughtful suggestions to help make the story more understandable. Finally, I would like to thank my family. Thank you for reading the story, expressing interest in my writing projects and for encouraging me along the way.

About the Author

Jasmine Fogwell grew up in the small town of Norland, Ontario. She spent many years living in a village in the mountains in Switzerland that inspired *The Fidori Trilogy*. She enjoys skiing, hiking, reading and writing.

About the Illustrator

Amanda Kramer Kaczynski is originally from Eugene, Oregon. She enjoys reading, travel, and meeting new people, as well as making art of many different kinds. She has also lived in the mountains of Switzerland, where she met her husband, Kyle. They live in Madison, Wisconsin

CPSIA information can be obtained
at www.ICGtesting.com
Printed in the USA
LVOW12s0615271016
510341LV00001B/6/P